D1058242

Krystal Ball is published by Picture Window Books,
a Capstone imprint
1710 Roe Crest Drive
North Mankato, Minnesota 56003
www.capstonepub.com

Cataloging-in-Publication Data is available on the Library
of Congress website.
ISBN: 978-1-4795-5875-9 (library hardcover)
ISBN: 978-1-4795-5877-3 (paperback)
ISBN: 978-1-4795-6198-8 (eBook)

Summary: Krystal Ball has a newfound power--she's able
to communicate with animals! Will this ability be a gift, or
will it lead to plenty of puppy problems? Follow the tale
of this fourth-grade fortune-teller to find out.

Designer: Kay Fraser

Printed in China.
092014   008472RRDS15

Krystal Ball

PET PSYCHIC

by Ruby Ann Phillips
illustrated by Sernur Isik

PICTURE WINDOW BOOKS

Table of Contents

My Future Awaits

Hi there! My name is Krystal Ball. I'm from Queens, which is a part of New York City. Some people call this place the Big Apple. But I live in a tiny, two-bedroom apartment with my mom and dad, so it seems pretty small to me.

Don't get me wrong . . . I *love* my parents. My mom works as a hair stylist on the first floor of our building. My dad's a high school history teacher. He's always saying things like, "History repeats itself, sweetie." Whatever that means.

I'm not that interested in the past, though. I'm much more excited about . . . the future.

I like astrology, palm reading, and stargazing. Why? Well, let me tell you a little secret. I'm not exactly normal. I may look small, you see, but I'm really a *medium*. That means I have a special ability, kind of like a sixth sense. My grandma calls this my "gift." It helps me see what the future holds, but it's never quite clear. I can learn things about a person or an object by touching them, and sometimes my dreams show little glimpses of events that haven't happened yet.

I usually have trouble understanding these visions, or premonitions, but I'm working on improving my skills. I also go to Nikola Tesla Elementary School, and being a fourth-grade fortune-teller while juggling science projects, math tests, and homework isn't easy.

What else can I tell you about me? Ah! My best friend, Billy, lives in the apartment above ours. I've known him my whole life, and that's a really long time. Almost ten years . . . Whoa! My other best friend, Claire, is the new girl at school. Both Billy and Claire know about my amazing gift, but they have pinky-sworn to secrecy.

Together, we zip around the neighborhood on our scooters, seeking out adventure. But with my abilities, adventure usually finds us first!

Okay, so you got all that? Good.

Now take a deep breath, relax your eyes, and clear your mind. My future awaits . . .

CHAPTER 1

ASAP

"Come over quick!" Claire cried on the phone. "The most amazing thing just happened!"

Then *click*. She hung up.

I stared into space for a few seconds before my brain kicked in and told me to *MOVE IT*! I jumped out of bed and started pulling off my comfy striped pajamas.

There goes my lazy Sunday morning, I thought.

It was my plan to stay in my room and read the new astrology book that I checked out from the library. My homework was finished, my chores were taken care of, and all that was left to do was fun stuff. Like reading about astrology!

But when your best friend calls and tells you to come over because "the most amazing thing" just happened, well, you drop everything.

I pulled off my pajamas, curled them into a ball, and threw them onto my bed. My shirt got loose and landed on Stanley's head.

Stanley is my stuffed Stegosaurus. I've had him as long as I can remember, which is, like, forever.

"Sorry, Stanley," I called out over my shoulder. "Now, what should I wear?"

I rummaged through my dresser and found my favorite purple tights at the bottom. I tried to pull them out, but they just wouldn't budge.

Suffering solar systems, what's going on in there? I wondered.

I reached into the drawer and tugged harder. The tights seemed to be stuck on something.

"If you pull any harder, Krystal, they'll rip!" I said to myself.

I've learned that it's best to say things out loud when you're talking to yourself. That way, if you actually hear it, you will remember it. Especially when it's going to keep you out of trouble or avoid a disaster like ripping your favorite tights!

I decided to pull the drawer out in hopes of discovering the problem. The clock was ticking, and Claire wanted me to come over ASAP. That stands for as soon as possible.

I jiggled the drawer left and right and up and down. Everything on top of my dresser clattered back and forth.

A heavy hairbrush tumbled off and bonked me on the head. Luckily, my curly hair is thick enough that it didn't hurt, but unluckily, the brush still got tangled in my unruly mane.

"Oh, this is ridiculous!" I shouted to Stanley. He still had the shirt over his head. Then I said, "It's a good thing you can't see how silly I look."

I jiggled the drawer harder, and the dresser banged against the wall.

Soon, there was a knock at the door.

"Come in!" I called out.

The door opened, and my mother walked in. Half of me was sticking out of the bottom drawer. The rest of me, meaning my arms and head, were on the inside.

"Good heavens, Krystal," gasped my mother. "What on earth are you doing?"

"Trying . . . to rescue . . . my tights!" I grunted.

When I pulled my head out, the cool air was a refreshing relief on my face. Frustrated, I blew the loose curls out of my face and pouted.

"Let me help you," Mom said.

In the blink of an eye, she reached under the second to last drawer, unhooked my tights from the loose screw they were caught on, and held them up for me to see.

"How did you do that?" I shouted with glee.

"You're not the only one with special gifts," she replied with a smile.

I gave her a huge hug, and she kissed my head. Then she removed the brush from my hair.

"So what's with all the racket?" Mom asked.

"Claire called and said the most amazing thing just happened. I have to get over there ASAP!"

I rushed to my chair and put on my tights.
Then I picked out a baggy sweater with a smiling
dolphin on the front.

"I love that sweater," Mom said. "Your father
bought it for you when his class went on a trip to
the aquarium."

"I love it, too," I said, looking in the closet.

I picked up my scarf box, turned it upside
down, and dumped all my scarves onto the floor.

"Krystal —" my mom protested.

I interrupted. "No time for neatness. I gotta
hurry!"

In the flurry, I found just the scarf I wanted.
It was purple and matched my tights, and it was
sequined and trimmed with gold fringe. I grabbed
the scarf and held it triumphantly in the air.

"Aha!"

Then I ran to my closet mirror and stopped
to look at myself. I carefully wrapped the scarf
around my head. One reason was to hold my hair
down, which was practical when you were riding
your scooter and wearing a helmet.

The more important reason was that I wanted
it to look just right. A little off center with the knot
tied under my left ear so the ends would drape
over my shoulder.

"There are some
things you just can't
rush," I said.

My mother glanced
around my room and
then looked at me. I
knew what she was
thinking before she
even said it.

"I'll clean it up when I get back!" I said.

Scrambling to scoop up my helmet and my scooter, I blew Mom a quick kiss and hurried out the door.

"Be careful, and be back for dinner!" Mom shouted after me.

I was out the door and headed toward the stairs when I crashed right into Billy.

Billy's glasses were knocked onto the ground. He put them back on to get a better look at me.

"Hmm . . . glittering tights . . . sequined scarf," he said, rubbing his chin. "You're off on another fashionable adventure!"

"I think so," I said and filled him in on Claire's urgent phone call.

At that moment, my body started to tingle. This usually happened when I was getting a vision or feeling.

I closed my eyes and tilted my head. "I'm getting a sensation," I said to Billy. "It feels warm and fuzzy like my favorite winter socks."

I opened my eyes and smiled. "An amazing adventure does await. It is decidedly so!"

"Then what are we waiting for?" Billy said. "Let's go!"

CHAPTER 2

Xena

Billy and I zoomed out of our apartment building and down the street on our scooters.

"Make way for the Human Torch!" Billy said, weaving in and out of the crowded street.

Claire lived only a few blocks away. Billy and I rode up 30th Avenue. The street had all sorts of fun little shops, including the bakery that Billy's parents own, House of Sweets. Everything in there is delicious! Even the napkins smell good.

Moments later, we arrived at Claire's house. Billy and I carried our scooters up the stairs and dropped them at the side of the door.

I rang the doorbell and called out, "It's me, Krystal! I'm here!"

"Hey, what about me?" Billy added.

As the front door opened, my body tingled again. I could feel danger was near . . .

All of a sudden — *BOOM* — something hit me!

A brown and white beast knocked me to the ground. I banged my head, scratched my elbows, and hurt my bottom.

Something heavy sat on my chest, and I couldn't breathe.

When I opened my eyes, a slobbering tongue was licking my face. The foulest stench in the history of the world filled my nostrils.

"UGH!" I cried in disgust.

The tongue started licking my face again. I put my hands on my attacker and felt soft, warm fur.

"Krystal, I'm so sorry!" I heard Claire yell.

The world was spinning. I didn't know which way was up or down, and my head throbbed.

"Oh, my stars!" I said. "It's I good thing I'm still wearing my helmet."

"You got a dog?!" Billy shouted. "That's so AWESOME!"

Claire and Billy pulled the pooch off me. I sat up and saw the cutest thing EVER looking back at me with a smile from ear to ear.

Even though my heart was beating faster than a rabbit's, it melted into mush.

I dusted myself off and got onto my feet.

The dog ran in circles, wagging its tail and sniffing our hands.

"Are you looking for treats?" Billy asked. "Hmm . . . I could go for some too."

"Marvelous moonbeams," I said. "Is this the 'most amazing thing' you had to tell us?"

"YES! This is it!" Claire exclaimed.

"Oh my!" I exclaimed. "She's the most precious darling I've ever seen."

"I know!" squealed Claire. "My dad adopted her from the animal shelter over on Steinway Street. It was the best surprise."

The pup scurried back into the house. We took off our helmets and shoes and followed her into the living room. She had jumped up into the lap of Claire's dad, Mr. Voyance.

"Meet the newest member of our family," he said. "This is Xena, our brilliant new beagle."

"Xena!" Billy exclaimed. "Like the Warrior Princess?"

"Yes, Billy," said Mr. Voyance. "You're absolutely correct."

Xena: Warrior Princess was an old TV show about a fierce fighter who used her strength and courage to help those in need. It took place in ancient Greece and came on after another show called *Hercules: The Legendary Journeys*.

Billy was obsessed with both shows. He owned every season on DVD. After we watched an episode, we would act out the scenes and make up our own stories.

I would play Xena, of course, because she wore purple and gold armor and had a sword.

Billy would be Hercules, the mighty mythical hero, and together we'd fight evil monsters.

When Claire moved to Queens, she got to play Gabrielle, Xena's best friend.

"That's so cool," I replied. "Xena the Warrior is my favorite. I like her because she's beautiful, and she kicks butt!"

Mr. Voyance laughed when I said that. "Yes, and that is why we gave our new dog that name," he said. "She certainly has the spirit of a princess and a warrior."

Xena must have agreed. She jumped up and gave Claire's dad kisses on his mouth and nose.

"Trust me, I know," I said with a nervous laugh and rubbing my sore bottom.

Claire giggled and clapped her hands.

The beagle bolted off the couch and bounded toward her.

"I want the two of you to start over and greet each other properly," she said.

I smiled and put out my hand.

"Nice to meet you, Xena."

The smart little puppy put her paw in my hand, and we shook.

Suddenly, a surge of energy coursed between us. I felt a wave of sadness and looked down into Xena's big brown eyes. Something was hiding behind them.

Claire and Billy saw my face change. I wasn't smiling anymore.

"What's the matter, Krystal?" they asked.

I tried to focus on the feeling, but it was fleeting. Then I turned to them and said, "Cannot predict now."

CHAPTER 3

Say What?

My thoughts were distracted when Xena jumped into my arms. She started licking my face again and rapidly wagging her tail.

"She's taken quite a liking to you, Krystal," Mr. Voyance said. "When I first met her, she was really shy and timid."

"Can you tell us how you found her?" I asked. I wanted to know more about Xena in the hopes that it would explain my vision.

"I was walking home from work today and passed by the animal shelter," Mr. Voyance explained. "I'd been thinking about getting a dog for our family because I had one growing up."

Xena curled into my lap. I rubbed her warm tummy, and she closed her eyes. It looked like she was smiling and listening to Mr. Voyance's story.

"As I walked by the store," he continued, "I saw this adorable puppy looking up at me. I couldn't say no to her."

Claire's dad smiled at the memory. "So I went in and asked about the dog in the window. The clerk told me that she had been found in a box outside the shelter."

"You mean, she was abandoned?" I asked. "That's so sad."

I couldn't help but think about the poor puppy, all alone, on a doorstep in the dark. It made me want to adopt every animal at the shelter.

Claire came over and pressed her nose to Xena's snout. They looked so cute together.

"I want a dog too!" I blurted.

Claire's dad laughed. "They're so darn cute, aren't they? But Krystal, owning a dog is a big responsibility. Isn't that right, Claire?"

"Yes, Daddy," Claire said. Then she looked at me. "Dad and I have come up with a schedule of all the things we have to do to take care of Xena. She needs to be fed, and housebroken, and bathed, and walked, and taken outside to poop."

Billy and I giggled.

"And then you have to pick up the poop!" Claire said.

"Ew!" I cried, pinching my nose. "How gross!"

"Well, the job *stinks*, but somebody has to do it," replied Claire.

We all laughed at her joke, and Xena joined in by barking along. *Ruff! Ruff!*

"Claire, honey," called Mrs. Voyance from the kitchen. "Please help me set the table."

"Okay, Mom," Claire replied.

As she got up to leave, Billy hopped up too. "I'll give you a hand," he said. "What's for dinner? I'm sure I can help with the leftovers."

They chuckled all the way to the kitchen, leaving me alone with Xena and Mr. Voyance.

I rubbed the dog's tummy and thought of ways I could convince my parents to let me get one too.

Then I heard a voice say, "I really like you!"

I looked around the room. Claire's dad was sitting on the sofa reading his newspaper. It couldn't have been him. It was a girl's voice.

"Did you hear that, Mr. Voyance?" I asked.

"Hear what?" he asked back.

"Nothing, I guess," I said.

I continued petting Xena and rubbing behind her ears. Her eyes were still closed, and she nuzzled her snout against my leg.

Then I heard the voice again. "You're so sweet!" it said.

It sounded like Claire.

"Thanks, Claire!" I shouted.

"Thanks for what?" Claire asked, sticking her head out from the kitchen.

I stared at her. "Didn't you just call me sweet?"

"No, I'm setting the table," she said, "and trying to keep Billy from stuffing the baked potatoes into his pockets!"

What was going on? I thought. *Am I crazy?*

"You're not crazy, Krystal Ball," replied the voice. "You're *special.*"

"AAAAGH!" I screamed.

Xena jumped out of my lap.

"Krystal, are you all right?" asked Mr. Voyance.

"Is your house haunted?" I whispered.

"Uh, not that I know of," he responded.

Claire, Billy, and Mrs. Voyance rushed into the living room. They looked concerned.

"Krystal, honey," Mrs. Voyance said. "You look like you've seen a ghost."

"I didn't see one," I cried. "I *heard* one. It spoke to me, *and* it knows my name!"

Claire and Billy giggled.

Looking up at the ceiling, I cried, "Are you there, Ghost? It's me, Krystal! If you're still here, say something."

"Something!" the voice said.

"There! Did you hear it?" I exclaimed.

Billy, Claire, and her parents exchanged looks.

"All we heard was Xena bark," Claire said. "I think you're spooking her."

"Don't be silly," the voice said. "You're not spooky. You're funny. I really, really like you."

Just then, Xena hopped into my lap and started licking my face. My brain was trying to make sense of what was happening.

"Xena, are you the one talking to me?" I asked the dog.

"YES!" she barked. "And I'm so happy to finally find someone who understands me, Krystal!"

I took a step back. My body started to tingle all over, and I felt sick.

"Krystal, are you okay?" Billy asked.

I looked at him and said, "I must have hit my head harder than I thought. Outlook not so good."

CHAPTER 4

Pet Psychic

I needed to leave Claire's house ASAP. My head was spinning, and I was going bonkers.

Can you imagine having a conversation with a dog? Sure, people talk to their pets all the time, but the pets don't usually talk back.

I smiled and said, "If you'll excuse me, I think it's time I went back home. I don't feel so good."

"Do you want me to call your mother?" asked Mrs. Voyance, looking concerned.

"Oh, no," I said. "I'll be fine. Thanks for having us over. Claire, I'm super excited about your pet. See you tomorrow at school."

Grabbing Billy by the elbow, I hurried to the front door.

"You're acting stranger than usual," Billy whispered as we put on our shoes and helmets.

"That's because things are stranger than usual," I whispered back.

"Oooh, how mysterious. Tell me everything!"

***

On the ride home, I waited until we were far enough from Claire's house before I told Billy about my *conversation* with Xena

He was silent for a moment, and then he practically burst. "That is so awesome. You can talk to animals!"

"Let's not get ahead of ourselves," I said. "Maybe I can only talk to Claire's dog. Maybe Xena is a spirit from a past life that's come back to haunt me!" I started to panic.

"Take a few deep breaths," Billy said.

"I know," I replied. "It's just that I have so much difficulty trying to control and understand my gifts, the last thing I need is another one."

"Oh, boohoo!" Billy said playfully. "I'm Krystal Ball, the Great and Powerful. Pity me for being so cool and amazing."

Maybe Billy was right. This could be the beginning of another exciting adventure.

Then suddenly, I heard another voice say, "Excuse me."

I looked behind me. No one was there.

"Watch it, will ya!" repeated the voice.

"Who said that?" I called out.

Billy stopped short and looked at me.

"Down here, Curly," said the voice.

I looked down and saw a pigeon pecking at my scooter. A piece of soft pretzel was stuck in the wheel. The bird was pulling it out with its beak.

"Are you talking to me?" I asked the pigeon, who was eyeing me up and down.

"Who else would I be talkin' to?" said the bird.

I gasped. Billy came over and put his hand on my shoulder.

"Humans!" the pigeon continued. "They never watch where they're going! They hog the sidewalk, they shove us out of the way —"

"I'm sorry, Mr. Pigeon," I stammered. "I'll be more careful next time."

Billy looked on, scratching his head. "Are you seriously talking to this bird right now?" he asked.

"What's it to you?" the pigeon snapped. "This is between me and Curly Sue. Mind your beeswax!"

My day was getting weirder by the second, and this mean little monster was making matters worse. "SCRAM, birdbrain!" I shouted.

The pigeon ruffled his feathers, grabbed the piece of pretzel, and flew off.

"Um, did you just get into a fight with a pigeon?" Billy asked.

"Well, he started it!" I cried.

The two of us looked at each other and burst out laughing.

* * *

Soon, we had arrived at the House of Sweets.

"This is my stop," Billy said. "My dad wants me to sweep the floors before he closes up."

"Okay, Billy," I said. "I've got to get home and eat dinner with my parents."

"Krystal," Billy said, "did it cross your mind that you can help animals with your new talent?"

"You mean, like Dr. Dolittle?" I laughed. "Don't be ridiculous. He was an old vet who learned to speak different animal languages. I'm just a sideshow freak that can read animal minds!"

"Then let's pitch a carnival tent and charge admission," Billy said. He climbed up on the bench outside the shop. "Step right up, folks, and meet the amazing Krystal Ball, Pet Psychic!"

"Will you stop that?" I cried.

Billy climbed down. "You'll feel better after dinner. I always do!" he said. "See ya at school."

I put my index fingers on the side of my head and closed my eyes. "Not if I see you first!"

CHAPTER 5

The Sphinx

That night, I was really quiet during dinner. My mind was replaying everything that happened.

"Krystal, dear, you barely touched your food," my dad said.

"I'm not really hungry," I mumbled.

"What was Claire's surprise?" Mom asked.

"Oh," I said, distracted. "She got a dog."

"That's wonderful," my mom said, trying to sound cheerful. "You both love dogs so much!"

"Is that why you're upset?" asked my dad. "I know you'd like a dog, sweetie, but I'm very allergic to them."

"I don't know if I want a dog," I said.

Mom and Dad exchanged looks. Mom said, "Krystal, sweetheart, do you want to talk about what's bothering you?"

I shook my head no. "Can I call Grandma?" I asked. "I want to talk to her about my gift."

For those of you who don't know, Grandma is *special*, like me. She can see the future too. Grandma helps me whenever I feel lonely or lost, and this is certainly one of those times.

"I'm sorry, honey, you can't," Mom answered. "Grandma is in Egypt."

"She's riding on a camel and going to see the Great Sphinx at Giza!" my father said excitedly.

"Do you remember who the Sphinx was?" he asked me, speaking like a teacher.

"Yes," I replied. "The Sphinx was a mythical monster that had the upper body of woman and the lower body of a lioness. Sometimes she had the wings of a bird and the tail of a snake!"

"Very good," Dad said. "She would stop people on their path and ask them a very difficult riddle. If they failed to answer correctly, she would gobble them up and spit out their bones."

"Oliver, please!" shouted Mom. "We're eating."

"So is the Sphinx," I chimed in.

Dad and I giggled together.

"The only person who could answer her riddle was Oedipus, the King of Thebes," Dad added.

I stopped smiling when the reality hit me. "So Oedipus could talk to animals?" I asked.

"I guess," answered Dad. "In mythology, anything is possible."

I don't know if that made me feel better or worse. This was real life, my life, not mythology.

* * *

After dinner, I headed straight to bed. Tucked under my covers, I hugged Stanley tightly. I tossed and turned until finally I fell asleep. But when I did, I had another one of my vivid dreams.

I found myself on a rocky hillside in ancient Greece. The area around me looked just like the pictures of ruins from my dad's history books. Only everything was still new!

Behind me, a temple with white marble pillars gleamed in the sun. Their reflection was blinding, and I had to lift my hand to cover my eyes.

The jangling of gold bracelets caught my attention.

I looked down to see that I was wearing several bracelets on both wrists. They were beautiful and had twisting, swirling designs.

They matched the gold sandals that were on my feet. The laces were long and twisted all the way up to my calves.

My body was covered with a white, knee-length dress that cinched at the waist with a gold belt.

I touched my hair. The long curls were pulled up onto my head and braided with a gold thread.

"Gosh!" I exclaimed. "I must look just like a Greek goddess."

I walked along a dirt road admiring the scenery, a dark shape flew by overhead. Suddenly, I heard a loud thud up ahead. Something big was blocking my path. It was hidden under the shadow of a large tree.

The figure looked like a tall woman, with long black hair and feathered wings on her back.

Could that be an angel? I thought.

The woman stepped out of the shadows. Her body was covered in golden brown fur. She had four legs with four paws just like a lioness.

"The Sphinx!" I gasped.

The Sphinx growled and chomped her teeth.

I screamed and ran down the dirt road.

I headed toward the coast and finally reached a quiet beach. There was nowhere to hide and no one to help me. I ran to the water and came upon a large open clamshell.

"Get inside," said a squeaky voice.

I turned toward the sound. The smooth, round head of a bottlenose dolphin was peeking out of the water. "I'm Fini," it said. "Hurry, there isn't much time!"

I climbed into the clamshell and found a long coiled rope made of seaweed.

"Throw me the reins," squeaked the dolphin.

"Is this some sort of chariot?" I asked.

Fini nodded. I tossed over the reins, and the dolphin looped them around her body.

"Hold on tight, dear!" she said.

I wrapped the rope around my wrists.

Without warning, I jerked forward and the clamshell was dragged into the water.

Fini's dorsal fin cut through the surface as we glided along the turquoise water.

"This is awesome!" I shouted.

For a moment, I had forgotten the danger I was in and enjoyed the amazing experience.

Then a dark shape blocked out the sun. The Sphinx had taken flight with her enormous wings and was now above me. I screamed again.

"Never you fear, dear!" Fini shouted.

The dolphin gained speed, pulling me faster and faster across the water, away from the sphinx.

The seaweed ropes started to burn against my skin. I held tight, but Fini was moving too fast.

All of a sudden, the reins snapped, and I fell backward into the clamshell.

"OOF!" I grunted.

Dazed and confused, I scanned the ocean for Fini. There was no sign of her. I called her name as loud as I could. "FINI!"

No answer.

I was alone again.

Except for the Sphinx!

I looked up, and the mean monster swooped down in my direction. She came charging with her paws extended. Those razor-sharp claws were coming closer and closer.

I shut my eyes and screamed.

CHAPTER 6

The Moon

"DON'T EAT ME!" I shouted.

I jolted up in my bed. Something was pressing against my neck. I gasped, but it was only Stanley!

Breathing a sigh of relief, I clutched the stuffed stegosaurus close to my chest.

"What a dream!" I told him. "I was certain that Sphinx would make a meal out of me."

I looked at the time. "Great galaxies! I'm late for school!" I said, rushing out of my room.

When I got to the kitchen, Mom was making breakfast. Dad had already left for work.

"Good morning, honey," my mother said.

She put a plate full of scrambled eggs and whole-wheat toast on the table in front of me.

"What happened?" she asked. "It's not like you to oversleep."

"I had a nightmare," I replied.

"My goodness! Do you want to talk about it?"

"I don't know what it means just yet," I told her. "I was being chased by the Sphinx, but then a dolphin came to my rescue. It dragged me across the sea, but then it got lost underwater and the Sphinx was about to eat me . . ."

Mom stared at me with a half smile on her face, nodding her head.

"I know what this means," she said.

"You do?" I asked, taking a sip of orange juice.

"Yes. It means I'm going to tell your father, 'No more mythology before bedtime!'"

* * *

After breakfast, I got dressed and met my mom at the door so she could walk me to school.

When we arrived, Mom kissed me on the forehead and said good-bye.

I ran up the steps into the building. As usual, Claire was there, waiting for me. Her curly hair was piled up into a bun, clipped in place with a plastic, puppy-shaped barrette.

The hair clip reminded me of what happened at Claire's house with Xena. I wanted so badly to tell her about it.

Here's a quick update: Claire had moved to Queens at the beginning of the school year. She was the new girl, and we hit it off immediately.

After a few months, I shared my biggest secret with her. I told her about my gifts and abilities. It was nice to have a friend that I could share this stuff with. I mean, Billy's okay, but sometimes he can be so immature.

Anyway, Claire didn't breathe a word. She thought it was neat to have a best friend with special powers. She acts like I'm a superhero!

"Hi, Claire," I said.

"Hey, Krystal," she said back. "What happened last night?

"Let's just say, we have *soooooo* much to talk about!" I replied.

At that moment, the bell rang, so Claire and I hurried down the hall to Miss Callisto's fourth grade classroom.

"Good morning, girls," Miss Callisto said with a smile.

Claire and I took our assigned seats. Luckily, our desks were right next to each other.

Once Miss Callisto had our attention, she announced, "This Friday is Show and Tell Day!"

The class cheered.

"Please bring in something special and personal that you'd like to share with us," our teacher added.

Claire's hand shot up.

"Yes, Claire?"

"Can I bring in my new puppy?" she asked.

"Of course you can," answered Miss Callisto.

"Yippee!" Claire exclaimed.

The rest of the class was thrilled. They asked Claire questions about her dog, and Miss Callisto clapped her hands to calm them down.

I got a little nervous. Aside from my special gifts and powers, I didn't really have anything special to share with the class. I wasn't going to stand up in front of the room and say, "Hi, my name is Krystal Ball. I sometimes have psychic visions and can now communicate with animals."

I closed my eyes and tried to concentrate. Suddenly, I had a great idea. My tarot cards!

They always help me in my time of need, and they are very special to me. I can bring those in for Show and Tell.

Tarot cards date back to ancient times. Grandma had given me a deck as a birthday present. She said that they would help me think and learn and, in time, show me the future.

You're probably asking yourself, "Can a deck of cards really do that?" They sure can!

While Miss Callisto moved on to fractions, I quietly opened my schoolbag and pulled out my tarot cards. I also took out a book of tarot card explanations that Dad bought me.

This first card I flipped over read **THE MOON**.

At the top was a yellow circle in a blue sky. Underneath were two dogs standing in a field. They looked as if they were howling at the moon.

Dogs, I thought. *How NOT surprising.*

I opened my book to the chapter on the Moon card and read its description.

The book said that
the card represents
sleep patterns.
Someone who gets
this card may be going
through a particularly
difficult time that can
put them in touch with
visions, insight, and
psychic powers.

Psychic powers? I gasped.

Claire looked over from her desk and saw
my cards and book. "This looks serious," she
whispered. "Is everything okay?"

I shook my head from side to side. "Cannot
predict now."

CHAPTER 7

Doggone It!

The school day passed in a blur. I tried to concentrate on the Declaration of Independence and photosynthesis, but it was just not happening. Billy's voice kept repeating itself in my head: "Krystal Ball, Pet Psychic!"

I was packing up my stuff when Claire and Billy came to find me.

"Hey, Krystal," Billy said. "What are you bringing in for Show and Tell?"

"Ask again later," I said with a smile.

"Ooh, Miss Mysterious over here!" Billy teased.

We all chuckled.

"Well, I'm going to bring in my rocket ship," said Billy.

"Is this the model rocket you got from the planetarium?" I asked. "I was wondering when you'd finish building it."

"Oh no, don't be ridiculous," Billy scoffed. "I took that thing apart and used the thrusters and blasters to soup up my model pirate ship."

Claire and I exchanged puzzled looks.

"That's right. I'm talking about space pirates! I don't think the world is ready for such genius."

Claire and I laughed.

"You're silly, Billy," she said.

"But very creative," I added.

As we walked toward the exit, Claire told us that her mom was coming to pick her up.

"And she's bringing Xena too!" Claire said.

We decided to wait in the schoolyard.

In the meantime, two sparrows flew over and perched upon a nearby branch.

"Is that her?" one said.

"It must be," replied the other. "That pigeon said she had hair that looked like a bird's nest."

"Hush!" said the first. "I think it looks lovely."

"Excuse me," the second one chirped. "Are you the girl that can communicate with animals?"

"Uh, yes," I replied, nervously.

"What's your name, little lady?" asked the nicer sparrow.

"I'm Krystal Ball."

Billy turned abruptly. "I know who you are —
we've been friends forever."

"Shh, you're interrupting," I said to him.

"Wait," Billy said. "Are you talking to these
birds too?"

"Pleased to meet you, Krystal," said the
sparrow. "I'm Janet, and this is Jack."

"Nice to meet you both," I said.

"Uh, can someone please explain what is going on?" Claire asked.

"This is what I wanted to tell you —" I said.

"She's a pet psychic!" Billy butted in.

"For real?" Claire exclaimed.

"Yep," I said. "It started with Xena, last night at your house. All of a sudden, she just . . . spoke to me, and I could understand every word!"

"You mean, when Xena's barking, she's really having a conversation?"

"YES!"

"Amazing!" said Claire. "I can't believe it."

"You can't believe it? I thought I was losing my mind, but I think it's all part of my gift."

"ACK!" Billy shouted.

Claire and I jumped with surprise.

A chubby gray squirrel landed in Billy's lap.

"Easy, mate," he squeaked. "I just want to get front row seats to meet Krystal Ball. I'm Pip."

"Well, it's really nice to meet you, Pip!" I said.

"Are you kidding me?" Billy exclaimed. "This is a scene out of a fairy tale! Are these guys going back to your house to clean your room?"

The squirrel looked at Billy sideways. "Nah," he told Krystal, "we only clean cottages with dwarves in them."

"Really?" I asked.

"No!" laughed Pip. "I'm just kidding, love! Tell your friend he watches too many movies."

I chuckled and told Billy what Pip said.

"This is unbelievable," he replied, shaking his head.

Mrs. Voyance arrived with Xena in tow. The happy beagle barked and wagged her tail.

"Uh-oh!" cried Pip. "DOG!"

The critters scattered and regrouped at the playground a few feet away.

"Hi, Mom!" Claire shouted. Then she said, "Drat! I forgot my Math book. I'll be right back!"

As Claire ran back into the school, Billy and I greeted Mrs. Voyance and gave Xena a pat behind the ears.

"Krystal! Krystal! Krystal!" Xena barked. "It's been so long since I last saw you. How are you? I've missed you."

She jumped up and licked my face.

"Oh, Xena, I've missed you too," I said.

I stood up and asked Mrs. Voyance if I could hold Xena's leash.

"Just make sure you hold on really tight," Mrs. Voyance warned. "Xena gets excited very easily."

"I will, Mrs. Voyance. Thank you."

While I walked Xena around the schoolyard, she sniffed everything in sight.

"I'm so happy to see you. I really like you. You're my friend, right?" asked Xena.

"Of course I am," I said.

"Well, you left before I could tell you something important."

"What is it?" I wondered.

Xena walked closer to the playground, and I followed.

"I need you to help me find somebody," Xena said. "Can you?"

"Sure," I said even though I wasn't. "Who are you looking for?"

Xena began, "I'm looking for — SQUIRREL!"

"Huh?" I managed to say.

"Squirrel!" Xena barked again, and then she jetted toward the jungle gym. She spotted Pip, and now the chase was on.

Uh-oh, I thought.

Pip jumped off the monkey bars and scampered across the playground. Xena picked up speed and dragged me behind her.

Thinking quickly, I ducked and narrowly missed the monkey bars.

Xena ran faster and faster, barking and panting.

I was panting too.

I suddenly got a feeling of déjà vu. You know, that feeling when you think you've experienced something before?

It was just like my dream, when I was getting dragged along inside that clamshell.

"Xena! Slow down, will you?" I pleaded.

"Come on, it's this way!" she cried. "I can smell him!"

As Xena ran even faster, the leash burned my hands.

I could hear Billy and Mrs. Voyance shouting in the background. They were trying to catch up to me.

"Xena, please stop!" I shouted.

Then I stumbled over my own two feet, tripped, and fell facedown in the dirt.

The leash slipped between my fingers.

The beagle bolted out of the schoolyard and onto the sidewalk.

Billy and Mrs. Voyance ran after her.

Quickly, I got to my feet. I ignored the wood chips in my hair, the scrapes on my knees, and the rips in my tights. I joined the chase.

When I reached Claire's mom and Billy, the N train had just pulled away from the station. A crowd of people came hurrying down off the elevated platform.

Xena became a brown blur bounding down the sidewalk. I could barely see her through the thick crowd. Frantically, we pushed passed them, but it was too late.

Xena was gone.

CHAPTER 8

Written in the Stars

Oh no, I thought. *This is definitely NOT good. This is a catastrophe!*

My body tingled. I closed my eyes and tilted my head. A cold feeling, like icy fingers, crept up and down my spine.

I turned and saw Claire standing under a tree. She was mad, for sure. With her black hair and angry face, she looked just like the Sphinx from my dream.

My body went numb. I gulped hard and wished right then and there that the earth would open up and swallow me whole.

"I . . . I'm . . . sorry," I croaked.

Claire slammed her textbook on the ground and ran to her mother. She started to cry.

I looked at Billy.

"Don't worry," he whispered. "You'll fix this."

"Don't count on it," I said. "This time I messed up royally. My gift is a curse. And it just cost my best friend her dog."

* * *

The car ride home was very uncomfortable. Claire sat in the front seat next to her mom, and Billy and I were in the back.

She was so mad at me. She didn't say a word or even look my way.

I would probably have done the same thing if I were in her shoes.

Claire's mom said that they would do their best to find Xena, and that because she had an identification collar, someone would contact them if they found her first.

I can't wait that long, I thought. *I've got to do something now!*

Mrs. Voyance pulled over in front of our building. As I got out, I tried to make eye contact with Claire, but she turned away from me.

I stood on the sidewalk, watching the car drive away. A million ideas were swirling through my head, but none of them made any sense.

Billy put his hand on my shoulder and said, "I know you're up to something, Ball, but it's always best to eat before going on another adventure."

***

When we walked into my apartment, Dad was already home. He was sitting at his desk grading papers. Mom was probably working downstairs at the hair salon.

"Hey, guys," he said. "How was school?"

I dropped my book bag and kicked.

"Never mind," Dad said and smiled.

He scooped me in his arms and planted a big kiss on my cheek. His mustache tickled. Then he tousled Billy's hair.

"Dad, something bad happened today," I said.

"Let me get us some milk and cookies, and you can tell me all about it," he replied.

"Whenever I'm in a funk, I choose double chocolate chunk," Billy said.

My spirits lifted a little once we sat around the kitchen table and started eating. Dad knew that my favorite cookies fixed me right up.

After I washed down my second cookie with milk, I told my dad everything that happened.

And I mean, everything.

Starting with the night I met Xena, including my new psychic abilities, and ending up with the horrible events in the schoolyard.

"Well, this certainly is a new development," he finally said. "Your gift, like you, is growing stronger. It's all part of what makes you special, just like Grandma. You'd be amazed at the amount of awesome things she can do."

"Really?" I asked.

"Oh, yes," Dad answered. "In time, you'll learn how to control them and use them to do great things the same way too."

"That's why I wanted to talk to her. I've made a huge mess, and I don't what to do," I said. "How am I supposed to find her in Egypt? She doesn't even have a cell phone!"

"You could send her an email," Billy suggested. "Does she have a laptop?"

"She's on a camel, Billy," I blurted out. "I don't think she can check her emails on a camel."

"Well, that depends," Billy said. "Does the camel have Wi-Fi?"

"Argh!" I shouted, throwing my hands in the air. "I might as well talk to the camel!"

Dad chuckled and lifted a dish towel off the counter. "I may not have the gift of sight like my mother," he said. "But I know a thing or two about giving advice. I did learn from the best, after all."

"Like what?" I asked.

Dad wrapped the dish towel around his head and puckered up his lips. He was pretending to be Grandma. Like me, she always wrapped her curly hair up inside a beautiful scarf. He looked so silly that it made me giggle.

"Everything is written in the stars," Dad started. He waved his arms wide and pointed at the ceiling.

"They have been consulted for guidance for thousands of years," he explained. "Sailors used them as a map to navigate the seas."

Billy and I just stared at him.

"What is he babbling about?" Billy whispered.

I closed my eyes and tried to see into the future.

"I don't know, but he may be right," I said. "Perhaps the stars will inspire me to find a solution to this major problem."

"Now you're babbling," Billy said as he helped himself to another cookie.

Getting out of my seat, I gave Dad a big hug and a kiss on the cheek.

"Thank you," I said to him. "You're the best!"

"So are you," he said back.

Then I turned to Billy. "Meet me on the roof after dinner," I told him. "I have a feeling those stars will give me a bright idea!"

CHAPTER 9

Calling All Critters

Later that night, I grabbed my telescope and astronomy book and headed for the roof. Billy was already there, waiting for me.

He was wearing a T-shirt of his favorite superhero show, Galaxy Guard. On his head was the helmet from his Galaxy Guard Halloween costume. Billy saluted.

"Galaxy Guard reporting for duty!" he announced. "What is our mission, Agent Ball?"

"Oh my!" I said. "What a pleasant surprise, Galaxy Guard. I was expecting my friend Billy."

Billy laughed and helped me set up the telescope. "What are you waiting for?" he said. "Let's save the day!"

I looked through my telescope at the billions of stars lighting up the night. Soon, I came across three stars in a row that glowed a bright blue.

"Ooh! I recognize this pattern," I exclaimed. "Have a look!"

While Billy peered through the lens, I quickly flipped through my astronomy book to the big constellation map.

"There it is," I said, pointing to the picture. "Orion's Belt!"

"Of course you'd recognize it," Billy said. "It's a fashion accessory!"

I rolled my eyes and continued to read aloud. "The Orion constellation is visible throughout the world. It's one of the easiest constellations to spot in the night sky. It was named after Orion, a hunter in Greek mythology. The surrounding constellations related to Orion are named after his two hunting dogs, Canis Major and Canis Minor."

I closed my eyes and tilted my head. Images started to swirl in my mind and come into focus.

Two dogs under the night sky, I thought. "The Moon Card!" I shouted, startling Billy.

"Excuse me?" Billy said.

"When I looked at my tarot cards the other day, I pulled the Moon Card. It's a picture of two dogs howling at the full moon. The first constellation we find is of a hunter with two dogs!"

"Great!" Billy cried. "But what does it mean?"

"I don't know," I replied.

Sliding down into the corner, I folded my arms over my knees and sighed. *What do the dogs symbolize?* I asked myself. *What is their purpose?*

"EUREKA!" I yelled.

"Stop doing that!" Billy shouted. "You'll give me a heart attack before I join the Galaxy Guild!"

"Orion is a hunter, right?" I explained. "That means I have to be a hunter!"

Billy scratched his head. "So you're going to get two dogs to find the one you lost?" he asked.

"Nope. I'm going to get creative and use another hunting party to seek out my prey!"

And with that, I cupped my hands around my mouth and yelled off the rooftop. "CALLING ALL CRITTERS!" I shouted. "THIS IS KRYSTAL BALL! PLEASE RESPOND!"

"You can't be serious," Billy said, grinning. "Oh, this is going to be good!"

"I don't even know if it's going to work," I said. "It was just a crazy thought."

I crossed my fingers, held my breath, and shut my eyes.

A few moments passed and nothing happened. I waited and waited and waited. Then, as I started to dismantle my telescope, I heard the pitter-patter sound of little feet scurrying up the side of the building.

Suddenly, a squirrel appeared and stood on the ledge. Next to it was a chipmunk.

"Hello, love," said Pip. "You rang?"

"WHOA!" shouted Billy.

"I hope you don't mind," continued Pip. "I brought a friend. This is Pia."

"Pleased to finally meet you," she said. "I've heard so much about Krystal Ball, the Great and Powerful!"

I blushed and told Billy what she said.

He let out a big laugh.

Suddenly, there was another sound — the fluttering of bird wings. Two sparrows appeared.

"Janet and Jack!"

"Hi, Krystal!" Janet chirped. "We came as fast as we could!"

"I can't believe it," I said. "This is amazing!"

"Believe it, kid," Jack snapped. "So why all the hullabaloo? I've got things to do."

"Hush, Jack," Janet said. "You can pick seeds out of your feathers later. Krystal needs our help."

"That's right," I said. "I need you to help me find my best friend's dog. She ran away!"

"You can count on us!" said Pip. The squirrel puffed up his chest and cleared his throat. "Listen up, gang. Janet and Jack will give us a bird's-eye view of the perimeter. Contact the pigeons if you need more eyes in the sky."

"Pia will call upon our tree-dwelling brethren, the chipmunks and the squirrels," Pip said.

"If I know dogs," he continued, "I'm certain one of our trees will be marked, and we'll be able to follow the trail.

"Lastly, I will cover the ground, questioning the alley cats and sewer rats. Those guys are everywhere, and they see everything. We'll find your pal's pooch, love. Don't you worry!"

Pip straightened his bushy tail and gave me a tiny salute. Then he hopped off the ledge and landed on a nearby telephone wire.

The sparrows chirped good-bye in unison and flew up into the night sky.

"Gosh," Billy gasped. "Do you think it'll work?"

I closed my eyes and felt a buzz in the air.

"Outlook good!" I said.

CHAPTER 10

Together Again

The next morning, I was sitting at the kitchen table with Mom and Dad. I could barely contain my excitement, so I woke up super early.

"How are you feeling today?" Mom asked.

"Much better," I answered. "Something wonderful happened last night!"

Before I could tell her, there was a tapping at the window. My mother pulled back the curtain and saw a sparrow pecking at the glass.

"Janet!" I shouted. "Open the window, Mom!"

As soon as the sill lifted, Janet flittered inside and perched atop the kitchen counter.

"Good morning, Krystal!" she chirped.

"Good morning to you," I replied.

Mom and Dad watched me speak with a sparrow that had flown into our apartment.

"Um, did I miss something?" Mom asked Dad.

"Yes, dear," he said. "I'll explain later."

"We have news about your friend's dog," Janet said. "We found her!"

"Splendid! Absolutely marvelous!" I shouted.

Overjoyed, I danced around the kitchen, kicking up my heels and twirling my arms.

"Thankyouthankyouthankyou!" I said again, petting her soft head with my finger.

"We must hurry," she informed me. "There isn't a moment to lose!"

I translated for my parents. As we rushed out the door, my parents and I heard screaming coming from upstairs.

"That sounds like Mrs. Katsikis," said Mom.

She was right. Billy's mom was hollering at the top of her lungs and stomping her feet but we didn't know why.

Suddenly, Billy came running down the stairs. Scurrying behind him were Pia and Pip.

"Howdy, folks!" Billy said.

"Oh, my stars!" I cried. "What happened?"

"Well, your furry friends here got the wrong apartment. As soon as my mom saw them, she freaked out. It was ah-mazing!" Billy laughed.

"She called us 'rats,'" Pip scowled.

"Well, you didn't have to jump on her head," Pia stated.

"Time is of the essence," Janet reminded us, and we followed her out of the building.

**

Moments later, Mom, Dad, Billy, Janet, Pip, Pia, and I hurried down 30th Avenue. A lot of the people heading to work and school were certainly puzzled by the peculiar parade.

"This way," said Janet. "We're almost there."

After a couple of blocks, we turned onto Steinway Street. Ahead of us was the Adopt-a-Tropp Animal Shelter. The shelter was named after the owners, Adam and Sue Ellen Tropp.

Suddenly, another sparrow fluttered toward us.

"There you are!" shouted Jack. "It's about time. I'm molting here!"

As we neared the store, I saw a familiar brown beagle with white spots standing with her front paws against the display window.

"XENA!" I cried.

"I'll call Claire's mother right now," said Mom.

Billy and I sprinted and hugged Xena. She licked our faces and wagged her tail.

"Krystal!" she barked. "You finally made it!"

"Oh, Xena, I'm so glad you're safe!" I said.

"Guess what!" Xena said. "I found who I was looking for!"

Then she put her paws back on the display window. Looking out at us from inside a cage was the mirror image of Xena. Only this beagle had white fur with brown spots.

She barked again. "I want you to meet my brother!"

"Your brother?!" I exclaimed in shock.

Billy pressed his face against the glass.
"Whoa. Now that you mention it, I see the family
resemblance!"

The other beagle wagged his tail and pressed
his snout against Billy's nose.

"I think he likes me!" Billy said.

I couldn't believe it. Everything made sense now. The two dogs from the tarot card, my new powers, everything. I was meant to help Xena reunite with her brother.

The realization overwhelmed me. Being a pet psychic actually worked!

"What are we waiting for?" Billy asked. He tugged on the store's front door, but it was locked.

"The shelter doesn't open until 8 o'clock. It's only 7:45," Dad said.

At that moment, the Voyance family pulled up in their car. Claire ran out, squealing with joy.

Xena leaped out of my hands and ran to her owner.

"How did you find her?" Claire cried.

I looked over at the crew of critters and said, "With a little help from my friends."

"Any time, love!" Pip said. "Our work here is done. Off we go!"

"Until next time," added Janet. "Good-bye!"

With that, my new friends scampered away.

Claire hugged me and apologized for getting mad. I said it was okay and that I would have felt the same way. Then I told her about Xena's brother.

"No way," Claire said. "Mom, Dad, Xena has a brother!"

We were all crowded around the window when a couple came up behind us.

"Can we help you?" said the man. "I'm Adam, and this is Sue Ellen. We're the Tropps."

Mom and Dad explained to them why we were all there. They were extra careful to leave out the part about my special gift.

While the Tropps unlocked the door, Mr. Voyance spoke quietly to Claire.

I couldn't help but overhear.

"Honey, I'd love to adopt Xena's brother and make him part of our family. But you know that our building has a one-pet maximum," he said.

Claire looked down at the ground. "I know," she said softly.

I wanted to help, but we couldn't get a dog either because of my dad's allergies. This happy day was starting to turn into a sad day.

Suddenly, we heard loud laughter and giggling coming from inside the store.

Claire and I ran over, and what did we see?

Billy was on the floor, and Xena's brother was on top of him. The dog was licking his face and wagging his tail.

"He likes him, Krystal," Xena told me. "He really likes him."

Then it hit me: a clear vision of the future.

Before I could say a word, Billy read my mind.

"I would like to adopt this dog!" Billy announced. "I mean, I'll have to double check with my parents, but how could they say no? I'm their number one son!"

"That way, Xena and her brother will be together forever," Claire said.

"Just like us!" I added.

"Of course, this strong and mighty beagle will need a name," Billy said. "I dub thee . . . HERCULES!"

Claire and I cheered.

Then we got on our knees to pat Hercules and rub his tummy.

"Thank you for finding me," Hercules said.

"You're very welcome," I answered back.

I was no longer surprised to hear an animal talk. I guess I was getting used to my new powers. And you know what? I was enjoying them.

"It's a pleasure to meet you, Hercules," I said. "Allow me to introduce myself."

"Oh, you don't have to," Hercules replied. "I already know who you are."

Now that caught me by surprise.

"You're Krystal Ball, Pet Psychic," Hercules said. "And wherever you go, adventure is sure to follow."

I smiled and exclaimed, "Without a doubt!"

Ruby Ann Phillips

Ruby Ann Phillips is the pseudonym of a *New York Times* best-selling author who lives in the Big Apple, in a neighborhood much like Krystal Ball's.

Sernur Isik

Sernur Isik lives in magical Istanbul, Turkey. As a child, she loved drawing fairies and unicorns, as well as wonderful, imaginative scenes of her home country. Since graduating from the Fine Arts Faculty-Graphic Design of Ataturk University, Sernur has worked as a professional illustrator and artist for children's books, mascot designs, and textile brands. She likes collecting designer toys, reading books, and traveling the world.

Horoscopes by Krystal Ball!

Astrologists believe a diagram of the position of stars and planets on a person's birthday foretells the future. This diagram is divided into twelve groups called *signs*. Find your sign and Krystal's prediction for your future!

ARIES (MAR 21–APR 19)
Krystal says: "Have you been bouncing off the walls with energy? Put it to good use and make something for a friend."
Lucky numbers: 9, 15, 33

TAURUS (APR 20–MAY 20)
Krystal says: "You are such a nice person to be around, Taurus. Your little acts of kindness bring a smile to everyone's faces. Keep it up!"
Lucky numbers: 2, 18, 49

GEMINI (MAY 21–JUN 21)
Krystal says: "Learning new things is your cup of tea! Don't be afraid to ask lots of questions. You never know what you'll learn."
Lucky numbers: 1, 24, 91

CANCER (JUN 22–JUL 22)
Krystal says: "Feeling nervous lately, Cancer? Don't worry — you are stronger than you know! You are totally ready for whatever comes your way."
Lucky numbers: 6, 21, 75

LEO (JUL 23–AUG 22)
Krystal says: "You're fearless in all that you do, and you love being the best. Remember to have some fun along the way!"
Lucky numbers: 12, 53, 67

VIRGO (AUG 23–SEP 22)
Krystal says: "Virgo, you've been feeling a little bored lately. Try playing some trivia and mind games to challenge your already brilliant mind."
Lucky numbers: 14, 36, 42

LIBRA (SEP 23–OCT 22)

Krystal says: "You're a natural people-person, Libra. You can't go wrong making a new friend!"
Lucky numbers: 4, 27, 83

SCORPIO (OCT 23–NOV 21)

Krystal says: "You've got tons of passion! Volunteering for something you care about is a way to channel your drive."
Lucky numbers: 3, 31, 62

SAGITTARIUS (NOV 22–DEC 21)

Krystal says: "Feeling blue? Put on your favorite tunes and dance! You will soon be feeling like your cheerful self again."
Lucky numbers: 19, 25, 64

CAPRICORN (DEC 22–JAN19)

Krystal says: "You're a hard worker, Capricorn, but don't be afraid to take a break. Try relaxing with a good book."
Lucky numbers: 15, 37, 80

AQUARIUS (JAN 20–FEB 18)

Krystal says: "You have been too cooped up recently. Get outside and explore the outdoors!"
Lucky numbers: 7, 38, 95

PISCES (FEB 19–MAR 20)

Krystal says: "You're good at caring for others, but make sure to make some time for YOU."
Lucky numbers: 20, 41, 73

Krystal's Fortune Game!

What you'll need:

- Markers, crayons, or colored pencils
- A square piece of paper
- One or more friends!

1. First, fold your square piece of paper diagonally in half to make a triangle. Make sure there is a crease. Then, open it up again.

2. Fold the paper diagonally the opposite way to make a second triangle. When you open the paper up again, there should be two creases in the shape of an X.

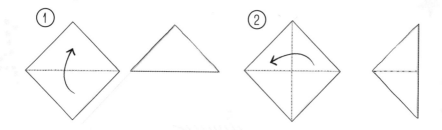

3. Next, take one corner of your paper and fold it toward the center. Repeat with each corner of the square. All the corners should meet in the center of the square.

4. Flip over the paper so that the folded side is facedown.

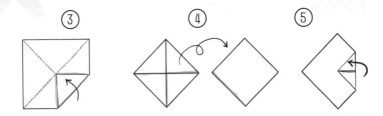

5. Repeat steps 3 and 4 to make a smaller square.

6. Keep the fortune-teller folded side up and write the numbers 1–8 in each of the creased triangles. There should be only one number in each triangle.

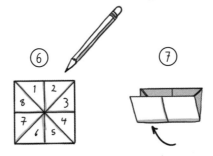

7. Open each flap and write a fortune on the inside of each triangle. You should have two fortunes written inside each flap.

8. Close the flaps back up, and flip the fortune-teller over. Now color each of the four squares a different color. Once you've colored them in, you're ready to predict the future!

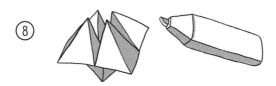

See what the future holds for . . .

Krystal ★Ball★

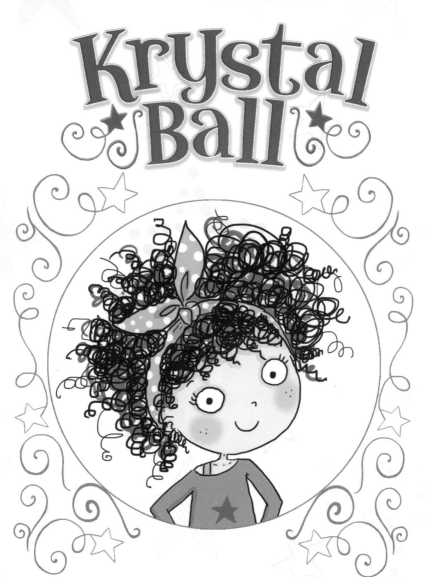

Read another book to find out!

Available from Picture Window Books
www.capstoneyoungreaders.com

THE FUN DOESN'T STOP HERE!

Discover more at www.capstonekids.com

Videos & Contests/Games & Puzzles
Friends & Favorites/Authors & Illustrators

Find cool websites and more books like this one at www.facthound.com.
Just type in the Book ID: 9781479558759 and you are ready to go!